Spike the Special Puppy

Karen didn't notice that Spike wasn't on the pavement beside her. Then a loud BEEP! BEEP! BEEP! made them both look round.

Spike had strayed a little further out into the road, and a motorbike was coming towards him, sounding its horn. But Spike didn't seem to have noticed it.

Titles in Jenny Dale's PUPPY TALES™ series

1. Gus the Greedy Puppy
2. Lily the Lost Puppy
3. Spot the Sporty Puppy
4. Lenny the Lazy Puppy
5. Max the Mucky Puppy
6. Billy the Brave Puppy
7. Nipper the Noisy Puppy
8. Tilly the Tidy Puppy
9. Spike the Special Puppy
10. Hattie the Homeless Puppy
11. Merlin the Magic Puppy
12. Fergus the Friendly Puppy
13. Snowy the Surprise Puppy
14. Bubble and Squeak
15. Crumble and Custard
16. Banger and Mash
17. Lily at the Beach
18. Lily Finds a Friend

All of the Jenny Dale's PUPPY TALES books can
be ordered at your local bookshop or are
available by post from Book Service by Post
(tel: 01624 675137)

Jenny Dale's PUPPY TALES™

Spike the Special Puppy

by Jenny Dale

Illustrated by Susan Hellard

A Working Partners Book

MACMILLAN CHILDREN'S BOOKS

Special thanks to Narinder Dhami

First published 2000 by Macmillan Children's Books
a division of Macmillan Publishers Limited
20 New Wharf Road, London N1 9RR
Basingstoke and Oxford
www.panmacmillan.com

Associated companies throughout the world

Created by Working Partners Limited
London W6 0QT

ISBN 0 330 48099 5

57986

A CIP catalogue record for this book is available from
the British Library.

Typeset by SX Composing DTP, Rayleigh, Essex
Printed and bound in Great Britain by Mackays of Chatham plc, Kent

Chapter One

"Spike! Get out of the flower bed before Dad sees you!" shouted Karen Truman, Spike's owner.

Spike was having a lovely time digging a big hole in the soft earth, and sending the soil flying in all directions. There were some very strange smells to investigate too. He sniffed at a pretty pink flower – and a black-and-yellow striped creature flew out. Spike yelped with fright and tumbled backwards, landing right in the daffodils.

"Spike! You bad boy!"

Just then, Spike noticed that Karen was standing behind him. He wagged his tail and woofed, "Hello, Karen! Have you come to play?"

But Karen was frowning crossly at him. Spike's tail stopped wagging. Uh-oh, he thought. I've done something wrong again.

Karen swept the puppy up into her arms. "Oh Spike!" she cried. "Dad's still mad at you for biting all the heads off his tulips!"

Spike nuzzled his wet nose into Karen's neck, hoping for a cuddle.

Karen sighed, then laughed. "Oh, Spikey – I just can't stay angry with you," she said. "But I *wish* you would do as you are told!" She hugged him tight.

Karen loved Spike so much. She could hardly believe it was only three weeks ago that she and her mum and dad had gone to Mrs Kelly's kennels to collect him . . .

They had driven out to the kennels early on a Saturday morning. Karen had hardly slept the night before. She was so excited.

The door was opened by James, Mrs Kelly's assistant. "I'm afraid Mrs Kelly's away at the moment," he said. "Her mother is ill and she's had to go and look after her."

"But she's arranged to sell us an Old English Sheepdog pup," said Mr Truman. "Will we still be able to buy him today?"

"Well . . ." James said, sounding unsure. "I've only been working here for a week and I haven't sold a pup before . . ."

Karen's heart thudded. She *couldn't* leave without her puppy – not when she'd been looking forward so much to getting him!

"But as Mrs Kelly has already agreed to sell him to you, then I'm sure it will be OK," James finished. "Let's go and take a look."

Karen sighed with relief and followed her parents and James out to the kennels.

Spike was chasing his brother Micky around the pen. His other brother and three sisters had already gone to new homes. The pen seemed quite empty now.

Suddenly Micky stopped and

stared over at the doorway. Spike turned to see what his brother was looking at. More people. Perhaps they would take either him or Micky away to live with them. Spike was quite excited about having a new home and an owner all to himself.

"Oh, there are *two* of them!" Karen gasped as James unlocked

the pen. "Mrs Kelly said she only had one for sale."

James scratched his head. "No, there are definitely two of them there."

"We can see that!" said Mr Truman, winking at Karen and her mum. James seemed very nice, but he wasn't exactly a bright spark!

Spike stared at the Trumans as they came into the pen. He decided he liked Karen's nice smiley face, so went over to say hello.

"Oh, this one's gorgeous!" Karen said as she bent down to stroke the shaggy black-and-white puppy.

Spike put his paws up on Karen's knees, wagging his tail as hard as he could. "You look very nice too!" he snuffled. Then he stretched up and gave her a big wet lick on the chin.

Karen giggled. "Both pups are really cute," she said. She tickled Spike under the chin, then scooped him up in her arms. "But *this* is the one I want!"

Now, three weeks later, Karen loved her puppy even more, but he could be *very* annoying when he wouldn't do as he was told!

"Spike, are you listening to me?" This time Karen tried to sound stern. "You *mustn't* dig up the flower beds!"

Spike peered up at Karen through the curtain of shaggy hair that flopped over his eyes. She seemed cross with him again, for some reason – and that would never do! So he gave her his best lick, right on the end of her nose.

Karen stopped frowning and smiled. Good! Spike thought. A nice wet lick always worked when the Trumans were cross.

"Hello, Karen." Mrs King, the Trumans' next-door neighbour, popped her head over the fence and smiled at them. "How's your new puppy?"

"Fine, thanks, Mrs King," Karen said politely. She liked Mrs King, but she could be rather nosy sometimes.

"I saw you taking him for a walk yesterday afternoon," Mrs King went on. "He's a lively one,

isn't he? You could hardly keep
up with him!"

"Well, he's only a puppy," Karen
said. But it was true that Spike
was rather hard to control when
she took him out. He never
seemed to do anything Karen
asked.

"Karen, time for lunch." Her
father came out of the back door

and beckoned to her. "Oh, hello, Mrs King."

"I was just telling Karen what a live wire her Spike is," Mrs King said. "He never sits still, does he?"

"No, he doesn't," Mr Truman agreed as Karen hurried over to the back door. She wanted to get inside before her dad noticed the damaged flower bed.

"We made it!" Karen whispered in Spike's ear, as Mr Truman turned to go back into the kitchen. But then a shout from Mrs King stopped him in his tracks.

"Goodness me!" Mrs King was staring over the fence. "Whatever's happened to all your lovely daffodils?"

Chapter Two

Karen's dad gave a loud groan.
"Oh no!" He rushed over to the
daffodils and began trying to
stand the broken stalks upright
again. But it was no use.

"Sorry, Dad," Karen said.

"Don't tell me – Spike!" her
father muttered, shaking his head.

"What are you looking so miserable about?" Spike yapped, and he leaned over and gave Karen's father a big friendly lick on the arm.

"Oh, get off, you silly pup!" Mr Truman said, but now he was smiling. Spike wagged his tail happily. He didn't like to see his family looking miserable – not while he had plenty of licks to go round!

They all went inside. Karen put Spike down on the kitchen floor and went to close the back door.

But Spike had other ideas. "Hey, I don't want to come in yet!" he barked, and he streaked past Karen into the garden again.

"Spike!" Karen yelled. "Come

back!"

Spike didn't stop. "Come and play!" he yapped. The door to the garden shed stood open, and he dashed inside to explore.

"Spike!" Karen called again.

"It's no use calling, he won't come back," Mr Truman sighed. "He'll be all right out there. Come and have your lunch."

Karen nodded, but she couldn't help feeling rather sad. Spike seemed to love her lots, but he *never* came when she called him. And why would he never do what she asked him to do?

"Sorry, Dad," Karen said again as they finished their lunch. "Spike really didn't mean to squash the daffodils."

Karen's mum shook her head. "I know he's only a puppy, but I didn't think he'd be quite so naughty," she said. "I couldn't find him the other day, even though I called and called. Then I found him behind the sofa, chewing one of my gloves to bits!"

"But *all* puppies are naughty," Karen pointed out. "They all chew things."

"Yes, but most do seem to learn their names quite quickly!" Mr Truman grumbled. "Spike *never* comes when he's called!"

Karen felt worried. She knew that her parents were fond of Spike, but it was true – he never seemed to take any notice of them at all! Karen's best friend Emma had a puppy too, called Daisy. When Daisy was told off, her ears went down and she looked ashamed of herself. Spike never did that!

"You'd better get Spike in now," said Mrs Truman as she stacked the dirty plates. "We're going over to see Auntie Ruth's new baby this afternoon."

Karen cheered up. She was dying to see her new cousin, Oliver, who was only three days old. Babies were just like puppies in a way, she thought as she went out into the garden. You couldn't tell babies what to do either! Anyway, she was sure that Spike's behaviour would get better as he grew older.

"Spike!" she called, looking round the garden. "Spike, come here, boy!" But there was no sign of the puppy.

Karen walked around the flower beds, looking among all the shrubs. She looked behind the compost bin and inside the greenhouse. Then she peered into the shed. Still no Spike.

"Karen, hurry up!" her mum called impatiently. "We're going to be late."

"I can't find Spike!" Karen called back, feeling worried. "Maybe he's got out of the garden."

"He couldn't have done," said Mrs Truman. "He must be hiding somewhere."

"Well, I can't see him," Karen said, biting her lip.

"Maybe you just haven't shouted loudly enough." Her father cupped his hands round his mouth and bellowed, "SPIKE! SPIKE! COME HERE THIS MINUTE – OR ELSE!"

"I should think you've just deafened all the neighbours!" Mrs Truman remarked.

Right on cue, Mrs King popped her head over the fence again. "Goodness me, what's all this noise?" she asked nosily.

"Sorry, Mrs King," muttered Karen's dad, looking rather

embarrassed. "It's just that Spike's gone missing."

"Maybe we shouldn't sound angry when we call him," Karen suggested. "If Spike thinks we're cross, he might not come out."

"That's a good idea," Mrs King said, folding her arms and preparing to watch what was going on.

"Spike, come here!" Mrs Truman called gently. "Karen's got a lovely juicy bone for you!"

Still no Spike.

They all hunted round the garden again, while Mrs King watched them. But there was still no sign of the puppy.

"SPIKE!" Mrs Truman finally yelled in frustration. "COME

HERE, YOU BAD BOY!"

"I thought we weren't supposed to sound angry!" Mr Truman remarked with a grin.

"Well, it's not making any difference, is it?" Mrs Truman sighed. "Where *is* he?"

"Maybe someone's stolen him!" Karen wailed.

"Oh, yes, there've been a lot of burglaries in the next road to this," Mrs King said helpfully.

"Maybe he went back into the house," said Mrs Truman. "I'll go and see."

"Did you look in the shed, Karen?" her father asked.

Karen nodded. "I looked in and called, but I couldn't see him."

"My friend's dog got locked in

her shed once . . ." Mrs King said, but no one was listening.

"We'd better take a closer look," Mr Truman said. "There are lots of places to hide in there."

After he'd nosed his way around the shed, Spike had felt rather sleepy. So he'd snuggled down in a cardboard box under Mr Truman's workbench. There was an old rug in the box and Spike had burrowed his way underneath it. Now he was having a lovely dream. It was raining bones, big juicy marrowbones, and Spike was running around catching them.

Then something touched him. Spike woke up suddenly. "What

was *that*?" he woofed in alarm. He shot to his feet, shook the rug off and charged out of his hiding-place in a complete panic.

"Dad, he's here!" Karen cried.

Mr Truman dived forward to catch Spike, but the puppy shot through his legs as he ran out of the door. "OW!" Mr Truman

tripped over Spike and fell on the ground moaning, "My ankle!"

"Dad! Are you all right?" Karen grabbed Spike and rushed over to her father, just as her mum came dashing across the garden.

Meanwhile, Spike nestled down in Karen's arms, feeling a bit guilty. He hadn't meant to hurt Mr Truman – he'd just got scared when he'd been woken up so suddenly.

"I think I've sprained my ankle," Mr Truman groaned as he climbed heavily to his feet.

"Oh no!" Mrs Truman rushed to help him, and so did Karen. Spike decided to help too. With a little whimper, he reached forward and tried to lick Mr Truman's nose.

But Mr Truman pushed him away. "Stop it, Spike!" he said crossly. "You've done enough damage for one day!"

Spike had never been pushed away before. He looked at the fierce expression on Mr Truman's face and cowered in Karen's arms. What was wrong? His licks had always worked in the past!

"Oh dear, what's happened?" Mrs King was leaning right over the fence in her eagerness to find out what was going on.

"I tripped over Spike and sprained my ankle," Mr Truman said shortly as he limped into the house.

"Oh, that puppy again!" Mrs King shook her head. "You know

what that dog needs?"

Nobody answered her, but that didn't stop Mrs King.

"Training classes!" Mrs King said triumphantly. "He needs to be taught how to behave."

Karen looked thoughtfully at Spike, and then she glanced at her mum. "You know, that's not a bad idea . . ."

Chapter Three

"I just hope this works," Mrs Truman said anxiously. It was a few days later, and Karen and her mum were on their way with Spike to their first training class at the local church hall. "Spike's been so naughty the last couple of days."

"He hasn't been that bad," Karen muttered. She still hadn't told her mum that Spike had chewed the corner of her new duvet to bits. Karen had told him off very sternly, but Spike hadn't even seemed to care. In fact, he'd ignored her and carried on chewing! Karen was pinning all her hopes on the training classes helping Spike to behave.

Meanwhile, Spike was sniffing his way happily along the street without a care in the world. He didn't know where he was going, but as long as he was with Karen he felt safe. Then he noticed a particularly interesting smell at one of the lamp-posts, and stopped to investigate further.

"Spike, come on." Karen tried to walk on, but Spike ignored her and wouldn't budge until she'd tugged at the lead several times. He didn't even look up.

"I just hope Spike behaves himself at the training class," Mrs Truman said nervously. "You know what he's like!"

"He'll be fine," Karen said, even

though she was worried too.

"Let's take him through the park so he can let off a bit of steam," her mum suggested. "Then he might not be so boisterous at the class!"

"Oh, great!" Spike woofed happily, as Karen led him through the park gates. He loved this enormous grassy place – there were so many interesting things to smell.

Because Spike never came back when he was called, Karen didn't dare let him off the lead. But she had an extendable one so that Spike could roam a little.

He was running about on the grass, his nose to the ground, when a man in a tracksuit jogged past. Spike didn't notice the jogger at all – until he ran right into the man's legs!

"Spike! Come here!" Karen yelled, struggling to reel in the lead. Spike tried to get out of the way, but only succeeded in tangling the long lead around the jogger's legs.

"Oi!" shouted the man crossly. He was so firmly tied up, he couldn't move a single step. "What's going on!"

Karen and her mum rushed over to free him.

"I'm very sorry," Mrs Truman gasped.

"So you should be," the man said shortly, then he jogged away as fast as he could.

"Oh, Spike, why don't you ever

look where you're going!" Karen groaned.

Spike whimpered. He knew he'd done something wrong, and he hadn't even been able to give that man a lick to say sorry!

"I'm a nervous wreck already, and we haven't even got to the training class yet!" said Mrs Truman. She sighed as they approached the church hall. "Maybe this isn't such a good idea."

The trainer, Mrs Davis, hadn't arrived yet, but there were several people with puppies already waiting outside the hall.

Spike's eyes lit up when he saw them. "Hello!" he woofed, and he charged forward, pulling Karen with him.

Several people began to smile, but a girl of about twelve, who was sitting on a wall holding the lead of a Labrador puppy, looked down her nose at Spike.

"Spike, stop it!" Karen whispered. Spike ignored her. He kept lunging forward, trying to get to the Labrador pup.

"Your dog's frightening Lucy," the girl snapped.

"Sorry," Karen muttered.

"He's not very well-behaved, is he?" the girl remarked rudely.

"Well, that's why we're here," Karen muttered. "There wouldn't be any point in coming to training classes if Spike was already well-behaved!"

The girl sniffed and looked the other way.

Spike was still struggling to get to the other puppies, but Karen kept the lead very short so that he had to stay close to her. Then suddenly, as Spike pulled even harder, Karen's hand slipped on the control button – and the lead shot out to its fullest extent!

"WOOF!" Spike barked happily. Free at last! He rushed forward to say hello to Lucy, the Labrador puppy.

As Spike shot towards them the girl screamed – and fell backwards into the flower bed behind the wall. She let go of Lucy's lead and the puppy ran off, as pleased as Spike to be free.

Everyone tried to help catch Lucy, but ended up bumping into each other. In the end there was a huge tangle of leads and madly barking puppies.

Karen finally managed to reel in Spike's lead again. Bright red with embarrassment, she turned to her mum. "Let's get out of here!" she gasped.

Chapter Four

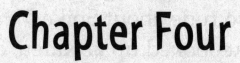

"What a disaster!" Karen sighed as she and her mum trudged wearily home again.

"I'm glad we left before the class started," said Mrs Truman. "I've had enough for one day!"

Spike was trotting gloomily along beside them. He knew he'd

done something wrong again, but he didn't know what.

Karen began to giggle. "It served that girl right though! She was so rude about Spike."

Spike looked up at Karen, and saw that she was smiling again. That cheered him up too. Whatever he'd done, it couldn't have been that bad! Wagging his tail happily, he began to enjoy himself, sniffing his way along the pavement.

"Yes, that girl *was* very rude, but unfortunately she was right!" Mrs Truman said solemnly. "Spike *is* awful."

"Maybe we could take Spike to classes when he gets a bit older," Karen suggested.

"Yes, but how do we know his behaviour is going to get better as he gets older?" Mrs Truman pointed out. "It might get *worse*!"

Karen frowned. "What are we going to do?" Then, suddenly, a nasty thought struck her. "Mum, you and Dad wouldn't make me give Spike away, would you?"

"No, of course not." Mrs

Truman slipped her arm round Karen's shoulders and gave her a squeeze. "We can see how much you love him."

"That's all right then." Karen felt very relieved. She couldn't bear the thought of losing her precious puppy, however naughty he was.

"We'll have to try and think of something else," her mum went on. "Maybe we could ring Mrs Kelly and see if she has any bright ideas. There might be some special training classes for extra-naughty pups that we can try!"

"Do you really think Mrs Kelly might be able to help?" Karen asked hopefully.

Mrs Truman nodded. "I'll ring her as soon as we get home."

While Karen and her mum were talking, Spike was trotting along the edge of the pavement, following a very interesting scent. It smelled like a couple of dogs had passed that way very recently. But then, suddenly, the trail changed direction.

Spike pulled on his lead and, to his surprise, it extended. He looked up at Karen. But she was looking at her mum, not him. So he moved off, in search of the scent.

Aha! Spike soon discovered that it had moved into the gutter. He stepped off the pavement to follow it.

Still talking to her mum, Karen didn't notice that Spike wasn't on the pavement beside her. But then a loud BEEP! BEEP! BEEP! made them both look round.

Spike had strayed a little further out into the road, and a motorbike was coming towards him, sounding its horn. But Spike didn't seem to have noticed it.

"Spike!" Karen yelled, yanking at the lead. She pulled the puppy to safety as the motorbike roared past, the rider shaking his head.

"Oh, Spike!" Karen swept the frightened puppy into her arms.

Spike lay against her, shaking with fear. What was that big machine that had nearly run over him? He hadn't seen it coming at all.

"Oh dear!" Mrs Truman looked

very pale. "You'd better carry Spike home, Karen. I think we've had quite enough excitement for one day!"

Karen was looking rather pale herself. A thought had suddenly struck her. "Mum! Did you see that? Spike didn't know that motorbike was coming – he didn't *hear* it!"

Chapter Five

Mrs Truman stared at Karen. "You mean . . . ?"

Karen bit her lip. "I think Spike might be deaf, Mum!"

Mrs Truman gasped. "*Deaf*? Yes. If you're right, that would explain everything!"

"Maybe that's why he doesn't

come when we call him, and why he doesn't take any notice of us," Karen said. "But how can we find out for sure?"

"We'll take him straight to the vet," Mrs Truman said. She stroked Spike gently on the head. "And if he *is* deaf, we'll contact Mrs Kelly as soon as we get home. She shouldn't have sold us a deaf puppy – not without telling us."

"I'm afraid this puppy *is* deaf," said Mr Fraser, the vet. He stood out of sight behind Spike, who was sitting on the table, and clapped his hands sharply three times. Spike didn't move or look round.

Mrs Truman sighed. "We thought as much," she said.

"Will he ever be able to hear?" Karen asked.

"I'm afraid not," Mr Fraser said. "It seems he was born deaf."

"But he must be able to hear *something*," Karen insisted. "He looks round sometimes when I walk up behind him."

"He probably feels the vibration of your footsteps," Mr Fraser explained. He banged on the table with the flat of his hand, and Spike looked round. "See?"

"But if he can't hear us, how are we supposed to teach him how to behave?" Mrs Truman asked, looking worried.

"There are ways," Mr Fraser

said. "I've got some leaflets about living with a deaf dog." He handed Karen and her mother some copies. "Why don't you read them and then come back for another chat?"

"OK." Karen picked Spike up off the table. She still couldn't quite believe that it was true. It was very upsetting to know that Spike had never heard any of the loving things she'd said to him, or even heard her voice at all.

Spike looked up at Karen. He could tell that something was wrong. And when he gave Karen one of his extra-special licks on the ear, she didn't smile at all. In fact, she looked even sadder! Spike couldn't understand it.

"I'm surprised to hear that you got the dog from a breeder," Mr Fraser went on with a frown. "They should have told you that Spike was deaf."

"Yes, they should," Mrs Truman said. "I'm going to ring Mrs Kelly as soon as we get home!"

*

"Dad!" Karen burst out as her father limped into the hall to meet them. "Guess what? We've found out that Spike is deaf!"

Mr Truman nodded. "I know," he said.

Karen stared at her father. "You *know*?" Puzzled, she and Mrs Truman followed him into the living room. A grey-haired woman was sitting on the sofa, looking rather worried. They didn't know who it was, but Spike did. It was Mrs Kelly from the kennels.

"Hello!" Spike barked happily. He liked Mrs Kelly, and he was very glad that she'd come to visit him in his new home! But why was she looking so worried?

"I got back to the kennels this morning," Mrs Kelly explained after Mr Truman had introduced everybody. "And when I found out that James had sold you the wrong puppy, I just had to come straight round and apologise—"

"The *wrong* puppy?" Karen asked, amazed.

"Well, yes." Mrs Kelly looked very embarrassed. "I knew that one of the two puppies left was deaf, so I wasn't planning to sell him. You were supposed to have his brother."

"Oh!" Karen looked down at Spike who was gazing from one person to another, wondering what was going on. "But what would have happened to Spike?"

she asked.

"I was going to keep him myself," Mrs Kelly said. "But when I got home, I soon saw that the wrong puppy was left. So I guessed that James had sold you the deaf pup by mistake."

Spike was beginning to feel rather worried by now. Everyone was very serious, especially Karen. What was happening? Maybe Mrs Kelly hadn't come to visit him. Maybe she'd come to take him back to the kennels! Whimpering, Spike pawed at Karen's leg until she picked him up.

"I'm very sorry indeed," Mrs Kelly went on. "And I've come to see if you'd like to swap the

puppies. Micky – the other pup –
is still available, and Spike can
come home with me."

Karen gazed down at Spike,
who looked back at her with his
trusting brown eyes. Did she
really want to change him for a
puppy who could hear?

Chapter Six

"No, thank you, Mrs Kelly,"
Karen said firmly, hugging Spike
closer. "Spike's a very special
puppy, and I want to keep him!"

"Well, if you're sure," said Mrs
Kelly, smiling. "He certainly has a
good home here." She reached out
to scratch Spike's head.

"Yes, we're sure," said Mrs Truman. "It's been difficult, not knowing Spike was deaf. We couldn't understand why he would never do as he was told," she explained.

"But now the vet has given us some leaflets with advice about living with a deaf dog," Karen added. "They should help."

Mrs Kelly nodded. "And you can take him to a trainer who knows how to work with deaf dogs," she suggested. "Deaf dogs can be trained just like hearing dogs," she explained. "But you have to use hand signals, of course. I'll give you back the money you paid for Spike, which will help you to pay for the special classes."

"Thank you!" Karen cried happily.

Spike saw that everyone was smiling again. Maybe he wasn't being sent back to the kennels after all. He was so relieved, he began smothering Karen in big sloppy licks.

"Stop it, Spike!" Karen laughed.

"I can see that he's very happy here," Mrs Kelly said with a smile. "He really loves you."

"I love him too," Karen said, hugging Spike even harder. It was a shame for Spike that he was deaf, but it made no difference to how much Karen loved him.

"Well!" Mrs King popped her

head up over the fence like a jack-in-the-box, and stared into the Trumans' garden. "What's going on here?"

"Oh, hello, Mrs King," said Karen. "Spike and I are just practising some of the things we learned at our special training class!"

It was a few weeks later, and Spike and Karen had already been to several training classes. It wasn't just Spike who was learning, either – Karen had found out lots of ways to help Spike.

"Do you want to see what we've been learning?" Karen asked. "Look!" She touched Spike to make sure that she had his attention, and then she gave the hand signal for "sit".

Obediently, Spike sat.

"Well, isn't that amazing!" Mrs King's eyes almost popped out of her head. "I'd never have believed it was the same dog!"

"Spike's doing really well at the class," Karen said proudly. "Mr

Lewis, the trainer, says that Spike's very intelligent!"

Meanwhile, Spike had got bored with sitting and had sneaked off to have a sniff around the lawn. He could smell something really delicious, and he wanted to find out what it was.

His nose led him straight to it – a big pile of bacon rind, toast crumbs and bits of biscuit that Karen had put out on the lawn for the birds. Lovely!

Just then, Karen noticed Spike wolfing down the bird food as if he hadn't eaten for days. She ran over to him, shouting, "Spike, leave!" then stopped, remembering that it would do no good.

Karen ran round in front of Spike so he could see her signal him to stop. But Spike carried on eating. It seemed that he hadn't noticed.

Then Karen laughed as Spike's tail wagged just a little. Perhaps he was pretending not to notice her as he hoovered up the last few crumbs. Perhaps sometimes – just sometimes – it was really rather useful not being able to hear!